What Will I Be?

Nandini Nayar
Francesco Manetti

KARADI TALES

It was hide-and-seek day. Amma counted to a hundred and came looking for Sameer. She saw Sameer's cap sticking out from the flowerpot, and she found him at once!

'I shall run away!' said Sameer, 'I will be an engine driver. I will take my train far away and you'll never find me!'

Amma laughed. 'But even trains stop at stations. And when you stop, I'll find you!'

'Then I'll become a pilot,' said Sameer, 'I'll be so high in the sky that you'll never reach me!'

'True,' Amma said. 'But even planes land at airports. And when you land, I will find you.'

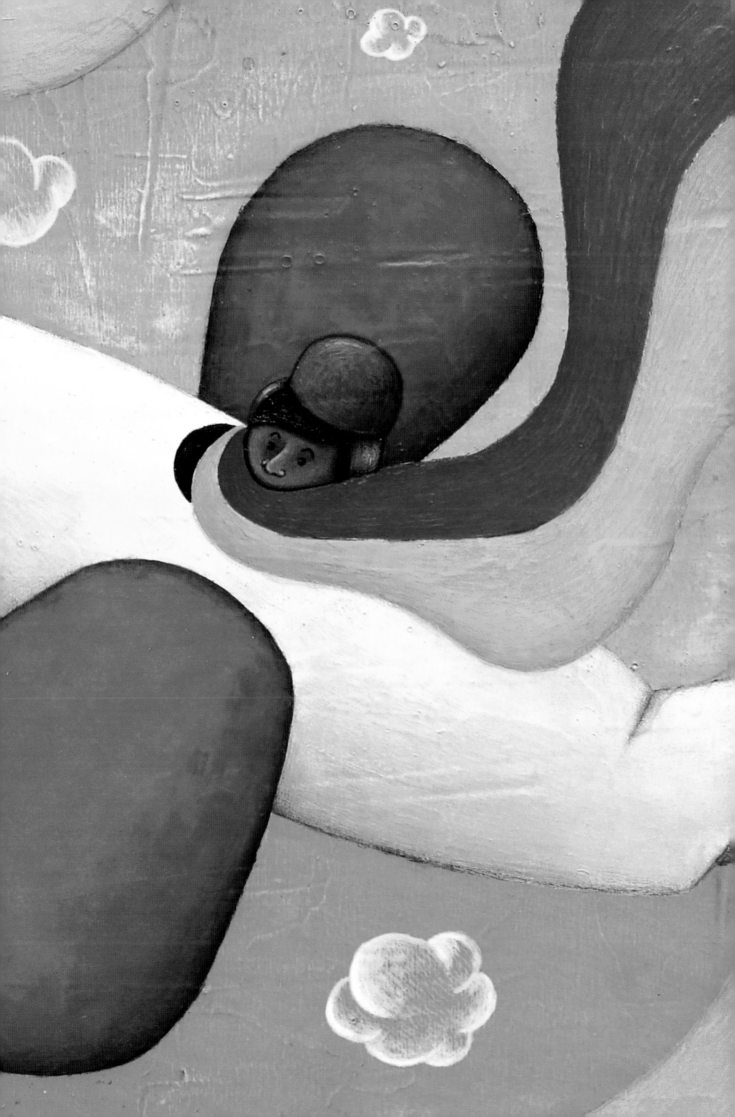

'Then I'll become a magician!' Sameer said, 'I'll disappear. Then you'll never see me.'

Amma smiled. 'But even magicians must reappear once in a while. And when you reappear, I will find you.'

'Then I'll become an ice-cream seller,' Sameer decided. 'I'll push my ice-cream cart far away and you'll never know where I am!'

'Ah, but even ice-cream sellers have bells on their carts,' said Amma, 'And when I hear the bell, I will find you.'

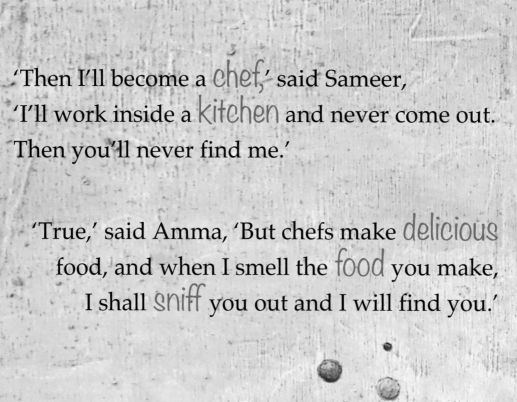

'Then I'll become a chef,' said Sameer,
'I'll work inside a kitchen and never come out.
Then you'll never find me.'

'True,' said Amma, 'But chefs make delicious
food, and when I smell the food you make,
I shall sniff you out and I will find you.'

'Then I will become a miner and go deep into the earth. How will you find me then?' said Sameer.

Amma smiled. 'You'll come up for sunlight and I'll find you at once!'

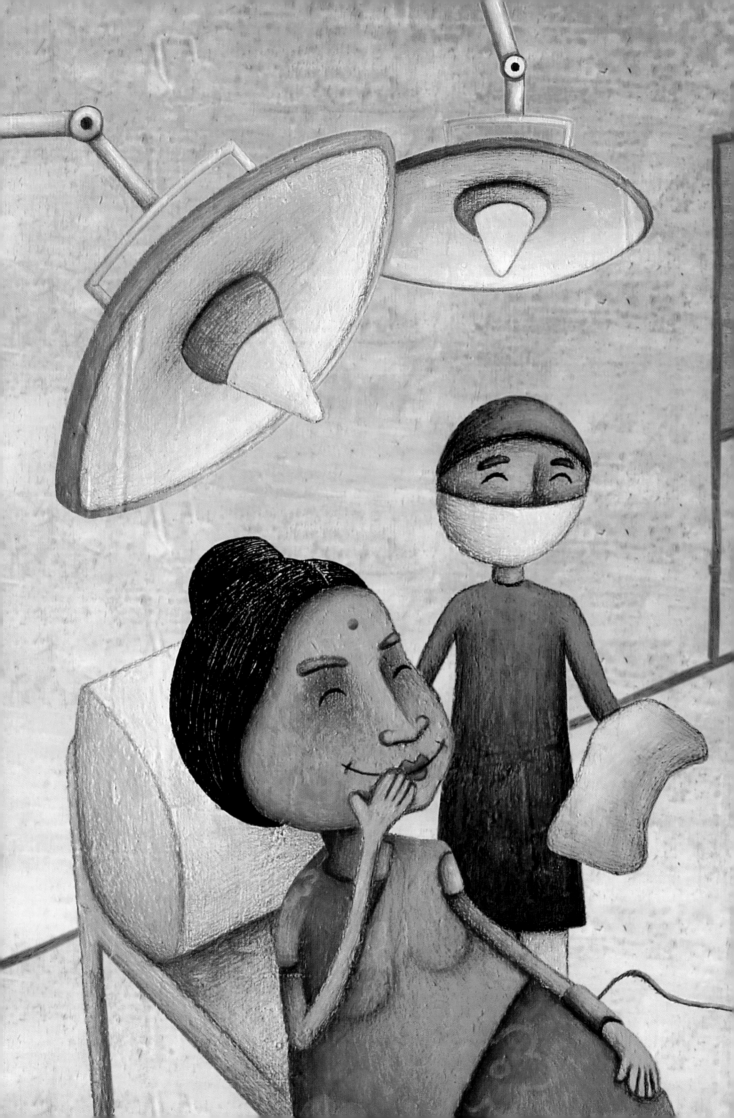

'Then I'll become a doctor. I will wear a coat and a mask and treat my patients. And you will never find me.' said Sameer.

Amma said, 'But if I fall sick and go to the hospital, you'll be my doctor, and I'll find you!'

'Then I will become an astronaut and fly away
to the moon,' said Sameer, 'And you will never
be able to find me so far away!'

'Hmm,' said Amma, 'When the moon is full
I will see you. Then I will find you!'

'Then I will become a mountaineer and climb high mountains,' said Sameer. 'I'll be so high up that you will never be able to see me!'

'Well,' said Amma, 'When you become famous and the newspapers write about you, I'll know where you are and I'll find you!'

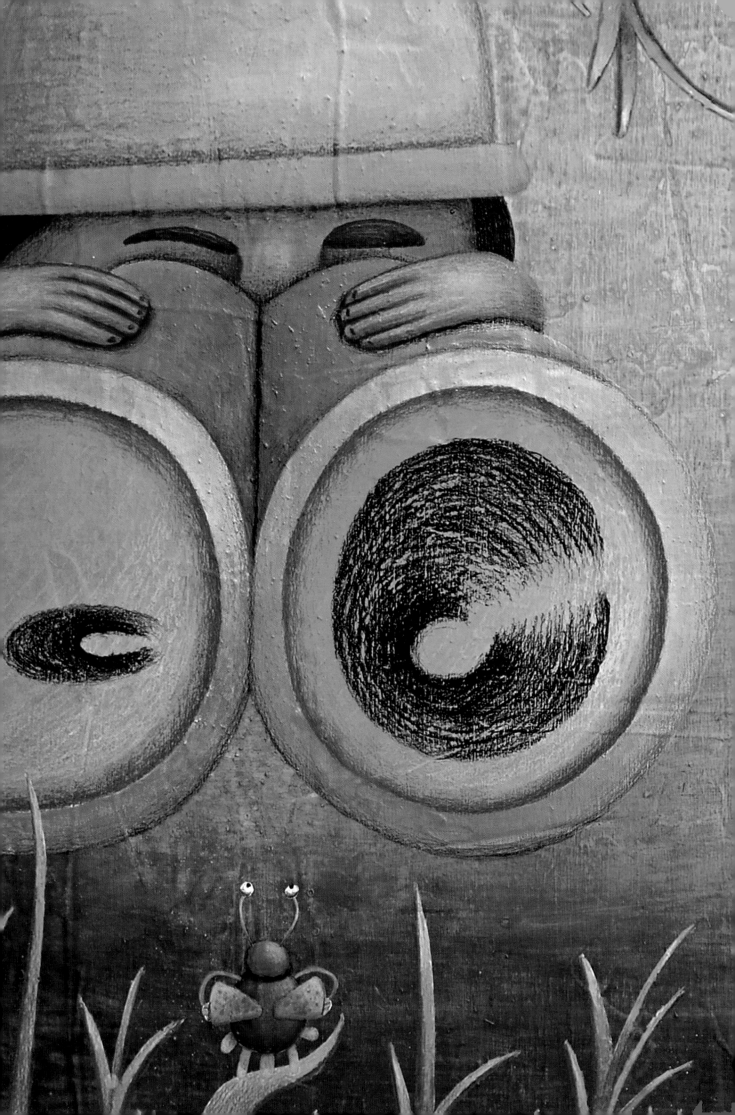

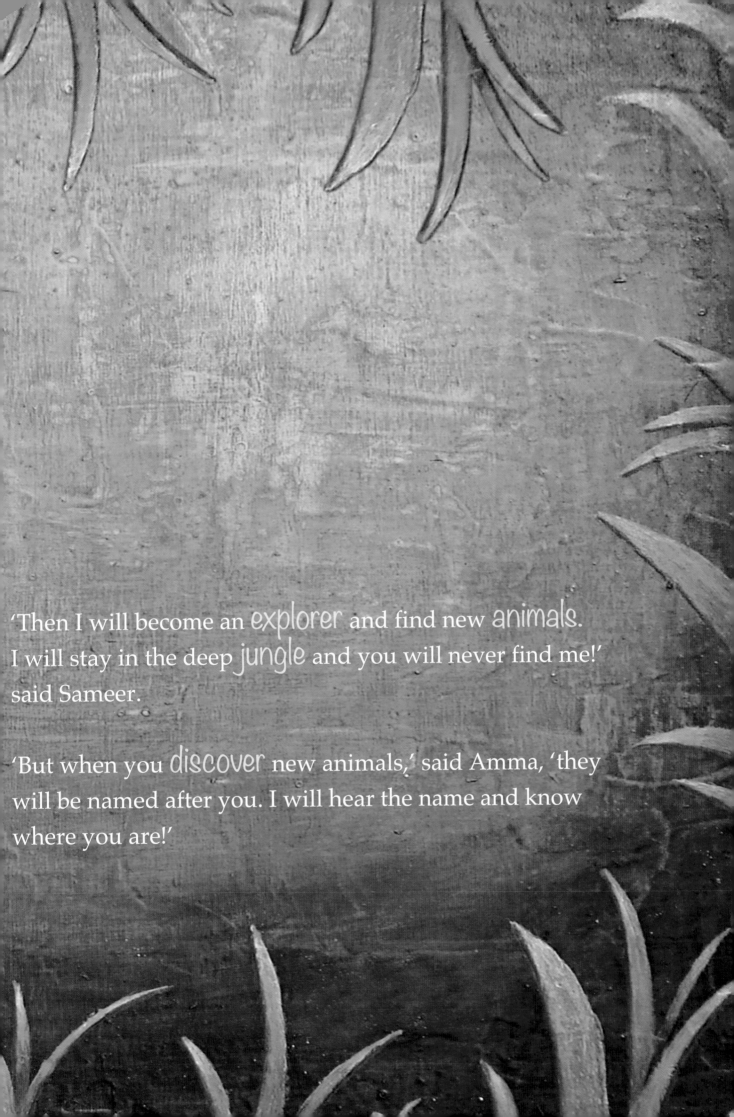

'Then I will become an explorer and find new animals. I will stay in the deep jungle and you will never find me!' said Sameer.

'But when you discover new animals,' said Amma, 'they will be named after you. I will hear the name and know where you are!'

'Then I'll become a zookeeper,' said Sameer. 'I will stay with the lions and tigers. Then you'll never find me!'

'What if the lion roars and the tiger growls?' asked Amma.

Sameer thought for a moment. 'Then I'll shout "Amma!" loudly.'

Amma laughed and laughed.
'Then that's how I'll find you!'

Sameer thought for a little while. 'I think,' he decided, 'I will stay with you a little longer.'

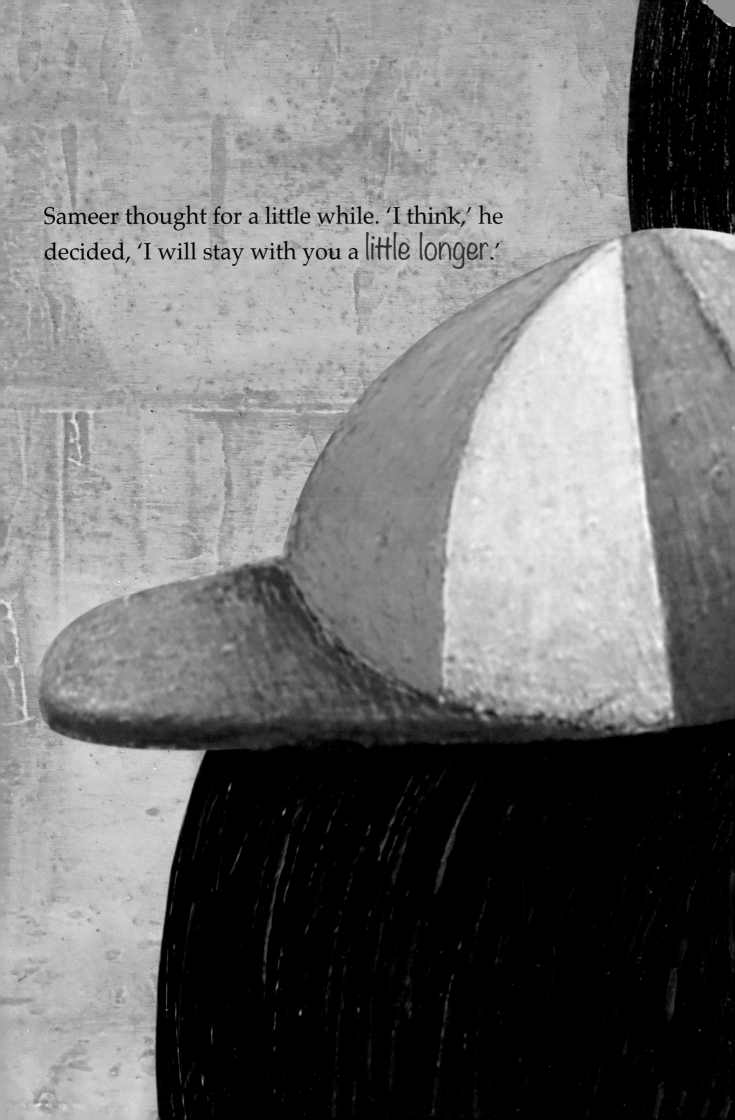

Also available in the
Curious Sameer
Series:

What Will I Be?

For Neeraj, in celebration of a wonderful childhood
— Nandini Nayar

Author: Nandini Nayar
Illustrator: Francesco Manetti

Karadi Tales Company Pvt. Ltd.
3A Dev Regency 11 First Main Road Gandhinagar Adyar Chennai 600020
Ph: +91 44 4205 4243 Email: contact@karaditales.com
Website: www.karaditales.com

Distributed in North America by Consortium Book Sales & Distribution
The Keg House 34 Thirteenth Avenue NE Suite 101 Minneapolis MN 55413-1006 USA
Orders: (+1) 731-423-1550; orderentry@perseusbooks.com
Electronic ordering via PUBNET (SAN 631760X); Website: www.cbsd.com

Printed in India
ISBN No.: 978-81-8190-284-9